Rory Branagan (Detective)
The Big Cash Robbery

by Andrew Clover
and Ralph Lazar

RORY
BRANAGAN
(DETECTIVE)

SEAMUS
BRANAGAN

STEPHEN
MAYSMITH

CASSIDY
CALLAGHAN

CORNER BOY
GILLIGAN

MIKE TYSON

MIKE
TYSON'S
BABY

DENT-HEAD
O'MALLEY

GUY 'THE EYES'
MURPHY

MICHAEL MULLIGAN

MRS
WELKIN

WILKINS WELKIN

NOAH THE NOSTRIL

MS
BIRKINSTEAD

SLUG LIP

FIONA
McTAVISH

KOMODO DRAGON

MRS
CHIPSTEAD

MR BOLTON

MR MEETON

MRS
DANIELS

DUNCAN
CLIFFHEAD

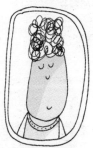

STEVEN
McEVER

NIGEL
BINAISA

Rory Branagan (Detective)
The Big Cash Robbery

by Andrew Clover
and Ralph Lazar

HarperCollins Children's Books

First published in Great Britain by HarperCollins *Children's Books* in 2018
HarperCollins *Children's Books* is a division of HarperCollins*Publishers* Ltd,
HarperCollins Publishers, 1 London Bridge Street, London SE1 9GF

The HarperCollins website address is
www.harpercollins.co.uk

1

Text copyright © Andrew Clover, 2018
Illustrations copyright © Ralph Lazar, 2018
Cover design © HarperCollins*Publishers* Ltd, 2018

ISBN 978–0–00–826589–2

Andrew Clover and Ralph Lazar assert their moral rights
to be identified as the author and illustrator of the work.

Typeset in Palatino Roman 14/22pt
Printed and bound in England by CPI Group (UK) Ltd,
Croydon, CR0 4YY

MIX
Paper from
responsible sources
FSC™ C007454

FSC
www.fsc.org

This book is produced from independently certified FSC™ paper
to ensure responsible forest management.

For more information visit: www.harpercollins.co.uk/green

Dedicated to all
kids who ride bikes,
and to all the people
who taught them how

I am Rory Branagan. I am actually a
detective.

Only one week ago, I – with my new best friend, Cassidy 'the Cat' Callaghan – chased down some POISONERS.

They tried to run, but we LEAPED in and *GOT THEM*.

Then we found some baddies hiding stolen dogs in a secret basement. But we *sneaked* in and *SET THOSE DOGGIES FREE*!!

Which was fairly *boomtastic*.

OK. You couldn't say for sure I'm the **biggest** *detective in the land* who deserves a *giant statue*.

But I'm definitely the *biggest one in my house*.

5

So you can *imagine* how I feel when I am climbing up to my *treehouse den* (with some chocolate, my dinosaur book and Wilkins Welkin, my sausage dog friend) . . .

and I find . . .

. . . my brother dressed like Sherlock Holmes!!!

'What are you *DOING*?' I say.

'Just drawing some of my *detective diagrams*,' he says.

I can't believe this. I am wanting to give him a *giant push right out of the treehouse*.

7

I am wanting to give him A GIANT PUSH OUT OVER A SWAMP!

SWAMP

9

'You will NEVER be a detective!' I roar.

'No, *you* won't!' he sneers. 'You're too easily *scared*!'

'YOU'RE too easily scared,' I say. 'You're even scared of SPIDERS!'

'I am *not* scared of spiders!' he says.

Right then, he *sees* a spider. He picks it up.

'I will even put it on my face!' he says. He puts it on his face.

The spider does nothing.

My brother *looks* like a giant spider, so it probably thinks it's safe.

My brother drops the spider.

'*You* would never do that,' he says. 'You are scared of *everything*!'

'I am NOT,' I growl.

'If a big, massive DINOSAUR appeared,' I say, 'I would touch *its* face . . . and then I would *ride* it . . .

'. . . and I would make it *chase after* YOU . . .

'. . . and then I'd make it BITE OFF YOUR *BIG HEAD* . . .

'. . . then *poo it out* INTO SPACE!'

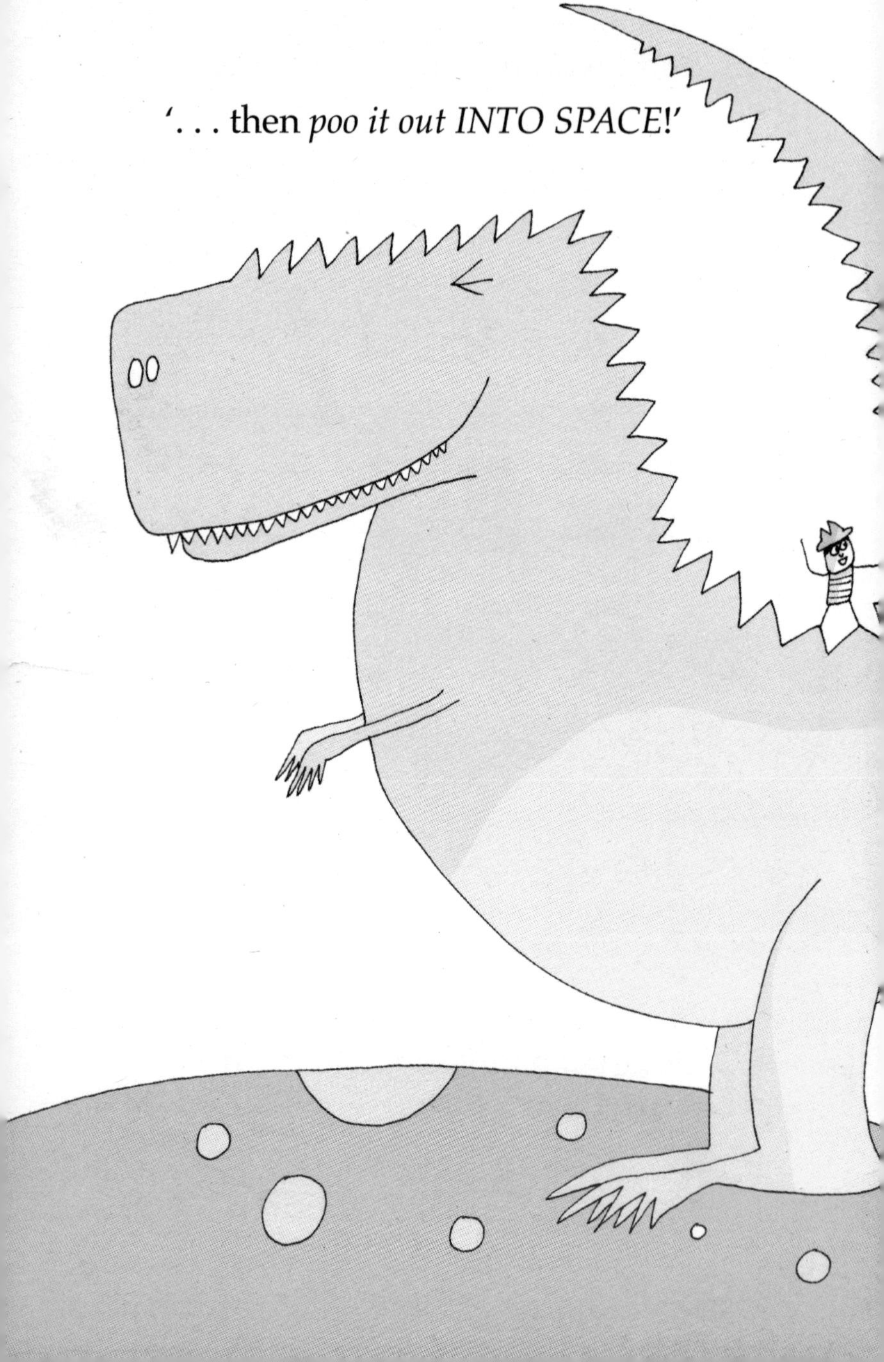

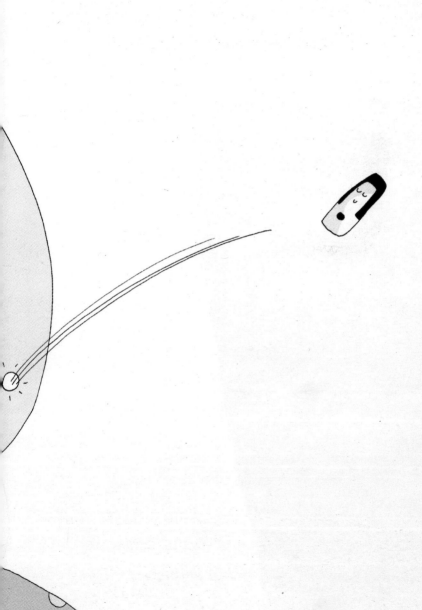

'*Huh!*' says my brother. 'You are scared of EVERYTHING! You are even scared of HEIGHTS!'

(I am not scared of heights. I'm scared of *falling*!)

'If even the tiniest dinosaur appeared,' says my brother, 'you would be so SCARED you would run off.'

'You're even scared of your *head teacher*!' shouts my brother.

I say nothing.

I am scared of ALL head teachers,
because their main job is to walk around,
like *velociraptors*, giving EVIL LOOKS.

But I am NOT admitting *that* to my
brother.

I just step forward
and poke him
in the chest.

'If YOU tried to keep up with my
detectiving, for even one day,' I say, 'you
would get SO SCARED, you would
RUN OFF CRYING FOR MUM!'

'I BET I WOULD NOT!!'

he replies.

And it is only *one day* after that, that my brother and I end up *finding a big, scary crime at my school,* and it involves *heights,* HEAD TEACHERS and SO MUCH *DEADLY DANGER* we would probably be safer being chased round a volcano by *velociraptors with HEADS LIKE HEAD TEACHERS.*

I'll tell you the whole story.

But, before I do, I must tell you about the schools in our town . . .

CHAPTER ONE:
The Two Schools

There is the King George School, which
is the *posh* school. It is next to rolling
hillside. It has a hundred buildings, which
have towers that are ten storeys high . . .

It also has *ten* football fields, and a *massive* swimming pool with diving boards, and twenty friendly ponies for the children to ride on.

And then there is our school,
St Bart's . . .

It's beside the old factory, and it has *one* building, and we have *one* animal – Mrs Chipstead, the school chicken, who bites children.

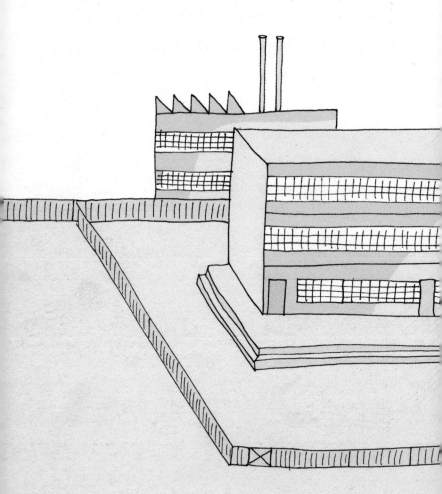

We also have only ONE football field, which has ONE goal with NO net, and it has a muddy puddle under the goal that is *so big* you wouldn't be surprised to see *crocodiles* hiding there, waiting to bite chunks out of the goalie's bottom.

We need repairs.

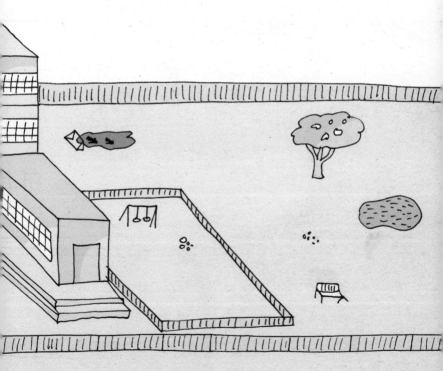

At the King George School, this would probably not be a problem. They would simply have a GIGANTIC SCHOOL FETE and there would be *bungee-jumping*,

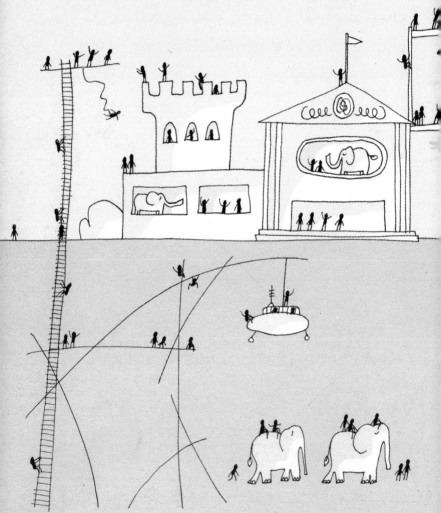

and *Olympic diving*, and free rides on an *elephant* or a *spaceship*, and they'd probably raise twenty-five million, and they'd repair *everything*.

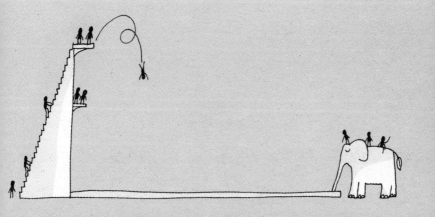

Our school fetes are just two mammies standing behind a pile of wet books. *No one* gets excited about them.

tissue

They're always raising money for stuff no one wants – like *safety equipment for the First Years' playground* – which we all hate.

As far as the rest of the school is concerned, the First Years should have *one giant swing* that should go *over a gorge* that's *filled with leaping crocodiles,* who should be allowed to eat one child each breaktime.

That is the world we dream of.

BUT THEN this year, our head went away for a special course. Her full name is *Ms Birkinstead*, BA, MA, NPQH (because she has loads of qualifications). But we call her *Ms Turkey-head* (because she looks like a turkey).

She left the school fete in the control of Mr Meeton and Mr Bolton, the deputy heads.

Mr Bolton likes grammar, telling you you're wrong and dunking biscuits in his tea.

He is an *eejit*.

But Mr Meeton is an absolute *legend* who could have been a rock star, or played ping-pong at the Olympics. (I know. I am *captain* of the ping-pong team.)

Mr Meeton started his first assembly with a huge *guitar solo* . . .

. . . and then he said he was in charge of how we spend the money from the next school fete. And he asked *US* what *WE* *might like to change in our school.*

Duncan Cliffhead stood up. He is a huge hairy boy in Year Six.

'We want a new football pitch!' he said.

'I don't like Mrs Chipstead,' said Amelia de la Court. 'Let's get a better school pet.'

'Guys,' said Mr Meeton. 'You are all thinking *too small*. What would you actually LIKE to see in this school?'

So then my good friend Corner Boy
Gilligan stood up.

'I'd like an ADVENTURE PLAYGROUND!'
he said.

Everyone went WILD.

'But what would the adventure
playground be like?' said Mr Meeton. '*Use
your imaginations.*'

Everyone turned to me, because
everyone knows I have the best
imagination in the school.

'It should be a HUGE climbing frame,' I said, 'in the shape of a *dragon*. It should

have a MASSIVE SLIDE coming out of its
mouth like a tongue!'

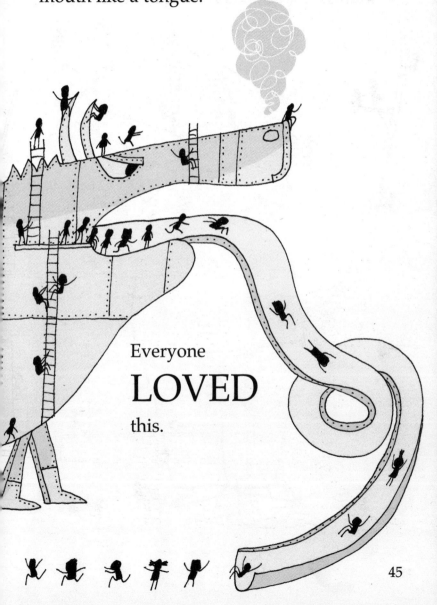

Everyone

LOVED

this.

Duncan Cliffhead stood up. 'My dad is a carpenter,' he announced. 'I bet he could make a climbing frame shaped like a dragon.'

'And we should also buy the Old Factory,' said Corner Boy.

'We should have *slides off the top*, and the bottom floor of the factory would be filled with *guinea pigs*, and then the next floor would be for *train sets*, and then the top floor would have a pool that would be *COMPLETELY FILLED WITH PENGUINS!*'

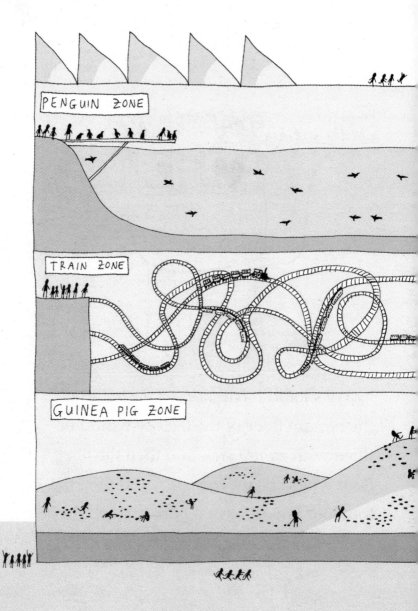

PENGUIN ZONE

TRAIN ZONE

GUINEA PIG ZONE

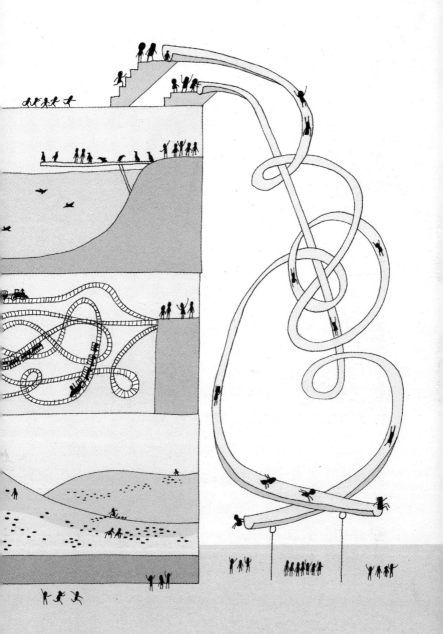

49

Mr Meeton stopped him. 'Guys! Guys!' he said (in his cool rock-star drawl).

'I'd say that an adventure playground climbing frame *might* be possible – though it would probably cost about ten thousand. BUT I'd have to say that one – penguins are *not* pets, and two – if we wanted to buy the factory, we would have to have *The Greatest School Fete of all Time!*'

So then Corner Boy stood up
on his chair.

'WHO WANTS TO HAVE THE
GREATEST SCHOOL FETE OF
ALL TIME?' he said.

Everyone went: 'YESSSSS!!!'

And then several people started to
chorus: *'Penguins! Penguins!'*

CHAPTER TWO:
Everything is Brilliant

That weekend we had the BIGGEST, BEST
school fete *the world has ever known*!!

We had sumo wrestlers.

A bouncy castle.

We had the World's Best Cardboard-box
Maze.

Corner Boy did guinea-pig racing.

We put a big stunt-man crash mat under the factory and people paid a tenner to *hurl themselves off*.

There was SO MUCH good stuff.

People were selling EVERYTHING. One guy sold the entire contents of his house. His sister was crying: *'Don't sell my Barbies!'* And so people started paying a tenner to buy the Barbies, then they *gave them back*!!

The girl cried, she was so happy.

Corner Boy shouted: 'If someone gives me a tenner, I'll sing *It Ain't Me* by Selena Gomez!'

Steven McEver shouted: 'I'll give you twenty, if you DON'T!'

Corner Boy shouted: *'It's a deal!'*

And fair play to Steven McEver – he paid up.

Mr Meeton held a massive line dance, and you could wear costumes from the drama department. A *stegosaurus* speared a dinner lady.

Corner Boy laughed so much he blasted *red lemonade* down his nose. I have literally never seen someone laugh that much.

My good friend Mrs Welkin came, bringing loads of cakes. I helped her sell them, and I am *proud* to say we sold every single slice.

(Fair enough, her cakes are delicious!)

Wilkins Welkin came. He took part in the dog race, and he got the special prize – a cake made from mince.

He hadn't won. He cheated and started about ten seconds early, but *no one* minded. Everyone *loves* Wilkins.

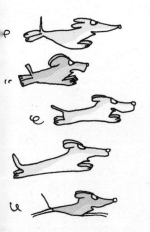

People came from all over.

The head teacher of the King George School came, who is Ms Birkinstead's sister. I looked up to see the poshest, scariest woman, who looked like Ms Turkey-head but with pearls and big hair, and I think she'd had plastic surgery because her top lip looked like a *slug about to burst*.

'Checking your sister's school's not *outshining* yours?' asked Mrs Welkin.

'*That* would never happen,' sniffed Slug Lip, walking off with her cake.

'Always jealous, that one,' said Mrs Welkin.

A black *Rolls-Royce* arrived. Two men in top hats got out. They opened the door to a *powerful*-looking man. He had a top hat on too. He also had *a Komodo dragon on a lead*!!

'Watch out,' whispered Mrs Welkin.
'That's Michael Mulligan the gangster.'

I was about to say: *How do you know?*
But then I just *looked* at the man . . .

If people were dinosaurs, he would be the
T-Rex – the biggest, the fiercest, the *king*.

I was just thinking: *Have I seen him before?* But then he walked to the line dance. He slugged down a drink, he

passed the lead to one of his men, and
then Michael Mulligan *joined the dance*.

Even the *Komodo dragon* had fun.
Someone got a hat on him.

We tried to get him to eat Mrs
Chipstead.

'He'll never get her in his mouth,' said
Corner Boy.

'He will,' said Nigel Binaisa (the cleverest boy in our year). 'The *Komodo dragon* can eat a whole goat. He gets his teeth round it, then – to stuff it down his mouth – he'll *charge* a tree.'

'That is when you KNOW you are trying to get *too much food in your mouth*,' said Nigel, 'if you have to charge a tree to get it down!'

Nigel pretended to charge a tree.

Everyone laughed. The whole day was *hilarious* – definitely the best day in the whole history of our school. *Everyone* agreed.

It all finished at 5pm, and then all the money was gathered up by Mr Bolton, who took it to Ms Turkey-head's office.

I watched through the window.

It took Mr Bolton ages. He gathered all the money into one of his biscuit tins, which he put into the school safe.

And then Mr Bolton came outside to *announce* how much we'd raised.

'We have all done *superbly* today,'
said Mr Bolton. 'And we've raised
five thousand, three hundred.'

We couldn't *believe* it. We'd not even
raised enough to buy the climbing frame.

We were *so disappointed* we just stood
and stared, as if we'd been turned to stone.

But then a deep voice *rumbled* from the back. It was the *T-Rex*.

'I would like to match the funds,' said Michael Mulligan. 'So the school has raised *over ten thousand* – which will buy you the adventure playground.'

'Why would he even do that?' I whispered to Corner Boy.

'Publicity stunt,' he whispered back. 'It's very important to make people think you're a nice guy if you're a criminal.'

'Are you *sure* about this?' asked Mr Bolton.

'No, I've changed my mind,' said the crime lord. 'I'll match your money with mine, but I'll multiply your amount by a *thousand*, so you have five-point-three *million*. You can buy the Old Factory at the same time. Call it the *Michael Mulligan Centre*.'

Mr Bolton couldn't believe it. 'Are you serious?' he said.

'I am *deadly* serious,' said Michael Mulligan.

'I'll be back on Monday morning at 8am, before school. I will bring along a large cheque. I will also invite the TV cameras. We will have a Big Presentation Event. You bring out your money. I will present

FIVE-POINT-THREE MILLION.'

No one could *believe* this. We were
going to get an adventure playground, a
factory filled with slides and we were all
going to be on TV.

'YESSSSSSSSSSS!'

roared the entire school at once, and we all
ran off, *filled with excitement.*

CHAPTER THREE:
The Cat's Pyjamas

On the day of the Big Presentation, I could not be more excited. I'll be going to school with Cassidy for the first time.

I just know she'll do something *amazing*,
and everyone will love her.

I hurry round to her
house before school.
Her mum lets me in.

'Hello, Cat!' I call up the stairs.

'Hello, DEADLY!' she calls back.

(That's what she calls me.)

I find her still in her pyjamas. '*Why* are you not dressed for school?' I ask.

'Life is one hundred and ten per cent better,' she says, 'if you wear your pyjamas all day.'

'And I have a very busy life,' she continues. 'I am not sure I have *time* to go to school.'

'You've not been yet,' I tell her. 'You *have* to go.'

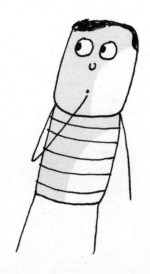

'We could just stay home and investigate your dad,' she says.

My dad disappeared when I was three.
Cat's helping me find where he went.

'I *want* to find where Dad went,' I say,
'but today we MUST go to school!'

'Very well!' she says, and she just
bounds straight out of the door, in her
pyjamas.

By the time I catch up with her, she's passing Mrs Welkin's house.

'There are some right *eejits* at our school,' I tell her. 'They'll take the mick, seeing your PJs!'

She turns on me.

'Are YOU scared of getting embarrassed?' she says.

'I'm scared of NOTHING,' I tell her.

'Good,' she says. '*Never* let yourself get embarrassed or you'll never be a detective.'

'A good exercise,' she says, 'is to be
EXTRA EMBARRASSING *on purpose.*'
I don't like the sound of this already.

'I suggest we YODEL loudly,' she says,
'while flapping like a duck.'

And that is why Cat Callaghan arrives at school, for her first day, wearing pyjamas and shouting: '*YODEL, YODEL, YODEL!*' while flapping like *a duck*. I am *terrified* people will look.

But they don't, because EVERYONE is in the playground, waiting for the Big Presentation Event.

CHAPTER FOUR:
The Big Presentation Event

Hundreds of people are there, all staring at a stage in front of the school, with a big screen behind. Two TV cameras are facing it.

It's one of those days when the sky is dark grey but the sun is beaming through in places, and you just feel *anything* could happen.

I am in detective overdrive. I'm looking everywhere, noticing everything.

I see Michael Mulligan's *Rolls-Royce*.

I see *Fiona McTavish*. Normally she's on TV reporting the news. Now she's on the stage, talking to Mr Meeton.

I see Ms Birkinstead inside the school, walking down towards the First Years' corridor. *What is she doing?* I thought she was on her course. And why would *she* not be talking to Fiona?

Michael Mulligan gets out of his Rolls-Royce, holding a big cheque.

Suddenly the big screen starts showing breakfast TV. I can see two presenters with bright orange faces, who are grinning away in front of pictures of our school.

You can *tell* any moment they're going to cut to here, and we'll be on TV.

Everyone goes quiet. The screen is showing Fiona McTavish holding a microphone.

The live filming has started.

'I am at St Bart's,' says Fiona McTavish, 'where the whole school has *come together* to raise money to improve the grounds . . .

'. . . I am here with the deputy head . . .
Mr Meeton – good morning.'

'*Good morning,*' says Mr Meeton.

'You must have felt very *proud* at the
school's efforts?'

'I *am* proud,' says Mr Meeton. 'I think
the whole school is AMAZING!'

'And we are going inside the building
to find the other deputy head, Mr Bolton,'
continues Fiona, 'who is going to bring
out the money the school have raised.'

One camera is now going inside the
school. On-screen, we can see Mrs Daniels,
the school secretary, in the front office.

We cheer.

Next on TV, we see Mr Bolton.

He smiles. Outside we all cheer:
'*Bo-o-o-o-o-olton!*'

He strides down the corridor towards
Ms Turkey-head's office. The camera
follows.

Mr Bolton goes into Ms Birkinstead's office and over to the school safe. He has to go round a pile of sporting equipment and shuffle round the school boiler. That's how rubbish our school is.

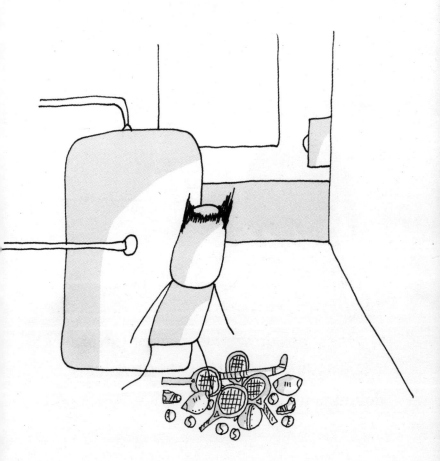

'And Mr Bolton will open the school safe,' announces Fiona McTavish, 'and bring out the money.'

Bolton opens the safe. He freezes.

'Mr Bolton?' says Fiona McTavish. 'Is the money there?'

He turns to camera.

'No,' he says. 'It's gone.'

'*What* is that you're saying?' asks Fiona McTavish (looking *very* worried). 'Are you saying someone has *stolen* the money?'

'It's not there!' he says.

'It appears a *crime* has taken place,' says
Fiona McTavish, turning to the camera
herself.

'And it seems St Barts is trying to turn
over a new leaf, but there's still some way
to go . . . Back to the studio!'

Outside, there's a stunned silence.

We cannot *believe* this. We were
supposed to be on TV, getting five-
point-three million and an adventure
playground. And actually our money's
been *stolen*, and the TV's now finished.

Suddenly there's a huge clap of thunder, it starts to rain, and everyone starts *running* away from the playground.

Cassidy is looking around at them. Suddenly she SPRINTS off. As I watch her, she goes *slamming* into a woman wearing a mac and a big hat who's just coming out of the First Years' playground.

I'm thinking: *WHAT IS THE CAT DOING?*

But no one notices. By now the rain is LASHING down. Everyone is *stampeding* to get out of the playground.

CHAPTER FIVE:
The Arrival of the Detective

*But this is how I know that **I am actually a detective** . . .*

While everyone else *runs away* from the crime, I *speed* towards it.

I sprint towards Mrs Daniels. I
commando-roll past her desk.

But the trouble is I was in bed last week
with a badly sprained leg, and a *blast of
pain* now *stops* me. *Owwww*.

And this is how I know that *Cassidy* is also a detective: while I am still twenty metres from the scene of the crime, arriving with a commando-roll . . .

. . . she just strolls through the fire-exit door and goes straight into Ms Turkey-head's office.

One second later, she's followed by
Mr Meeton and Mr Bolton, and they're
all followed by *Stephen Maysmith*, the big
police detective, who comes charging after
them like a big *Inspectosaurus*.

Mrs Daniels comes hurrying past too.

I can't believe this. Even *Mrs Daniels* is
beating me to the scene of the crime.

Hobbling over, I peek round the opened door of Ms Turkey-head's office. I *notice* a dent in it, about half a metre off the floor.

Cassidy's on the Turkey's desk, peering into the safe.

'*Who are you?*' asks Mr Meeton.

'I am Cassidy Callaghan,' she says, 'reporting for my first day.'

'I think we have FOUND our culprit,' says Mr Bolton. He turns to Stephen Maysmith. *'Officer, arrest that child.'*

The *Inspectosaurus* reaches out to grab the Cat. But she then does something *amazing . . .*

. . . She *springs* away from Maysmith.

She *leaps* on to the boiler.

She jumps, then . . .

. . . soars, somersaulting *over the people . . .*

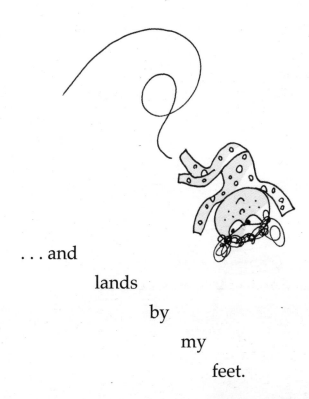

. . . and

      lands

           by

               my

                  feet.

'Mr Detective,' she whispers. 'Take that.'
She puts something in my hand.

She says, 'It seems we have a *crime* to
solve.' And she smiles.

And so now I am still very *angry* that someone has *stolen our money*. But still I LOVE IT that the great *crime-fighting* DUO are back together!

I'm thinking: *It's another case for Cat and Deadly!!*

But Mr Maysmith's thinking: *That girl's suspicious!* And he *rugby-tackles* her to the floor.

'Don't be STUPID!' I shout. 'There is no way SHE took that money!'

But Stephen Maysmith just PULLS her to her feet and he leads my friend away.

I am wanting to *charge* after him and get her back.

But my way is blocked by Mr Bolton.

'The school is now CLOSED,' he warns,
'for a POLICE INVESTIGATION. Go
straight home.'

CHAPTER SIX:
Investigation

Soon after, I'm back home, in my room, and I am ANGRY. I cannot BELIEVE someone has done a CRIME at our school, and I can't believe Cat is being BLAMED for it.

I am feeling that I am on thin ice, over a deep, deep lake that is filled with monsters, and the person who normally helps me is GONE.

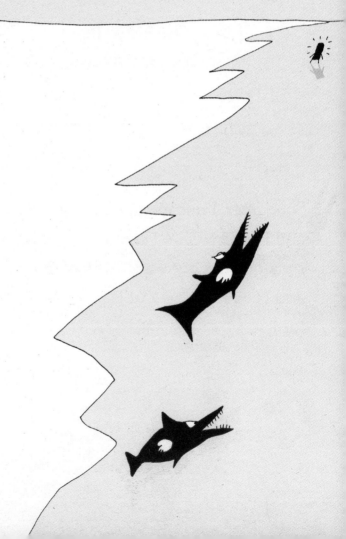

I *wish* Cassidy was here.

Then I think, if she were, she'd say, 'MASTER YOUR EMOTIONS, and INVESTIGATE THE FACTS.'

And I realise that I have an important clue that she gave me before she was taken. I find it.

It's a memory stick. It has a piece of paper Sellotaped on, which says *CCTV*. I get Mum's laptop.

I push the memory stick in and press
play.

I just see Ms Turkey-head coming
gobbling into her office, over and over,
holding coffee. I fast-forward. I see Bolton
come galloping in (holding tea). Then the
footage gets stuck and I can't budge it on.
When I press, it keeps saying: *Record*.

Then I start to get annoyed, so I record myself saying: '*I am the Bolton Man . . . I stole the money and dunked it in my tea!*'

That makes me laugh. So then I make up a rap. I go: '*Big Bad Bolton Man! I said Big Bad Bolton Man! (Uh huh huh.)*'

Then I just mess about.

I turn the laptop upside down, so I look like a lizard hanging from the ceiling who's going: '*Big Bad Bolton Man . . . I say YOU, my Bolton Man! (Oh yeah!)*'

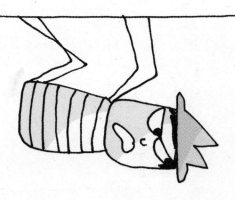

Then my brother comes in.

'*What* are you doing?' he says.

I say nothing. Suddenly he springs forward and grabs the computer.

Luckily, he can't see me being a lizard.
He just sees Ms Turkey-head going into
the office.

'You've got important EVIDENCE from the crime at the school!' he says. 'Why have you GOT this?'

'Because I am trying to find out who took the money.'

'But you can't take IMPORTANT EVIDENCE that *the police* will need,' he says.

I say nothing. I'm starting to feel guilty.

'I hope you haven't *messed* with this!'
he says.

I say nothing.

No one can make me feel guilty like my
brother.

Already I am slithering in a big SWAMP OF SHAME and *the GUILT MONSTERS are biting.*

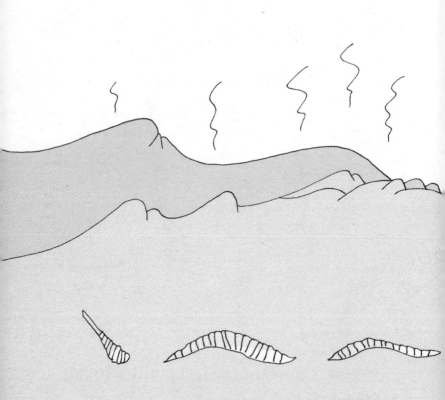

I *hate* him now.

'You could go to *prison* for interfering with a police investigation,' he says. 'You must put this straight back where it came from . . .'

Then he gives me an *evil* smile.

'. . . Except you'd be too *scared* to do it,' he says.

'I WOULDN'T be scared to do that,' I say. 'YOU would!'

'I would NOT!' says my brother. 'I'd *happily* come.'

I start to smile.

I realise he is *so jealous* of my *detectiving*, he wants to come with me. And I realise that having my eejit brother is not NEARLY as good as having Cat. But it's better than nothing.

'How will we get there?' I ask.

'*I* reckon,' he says, 'we should take the bikes.'

I snort at that. My brother is OBSESSED with his new bike. He has the whole bike outfit. He rushes off to put it on.

So now he looks like a big spider that
has a mushroom on his head and is
wearing tight black shorts.

I go outside.

And that's where I see Corner Boy. He's getting his bike out too. He sees me.

'Rory!' he shouts. 'I AM VERY WORRIED ABOUT MIKE TYSON'S BABY!'

Corner Boy is *always* talking about his favourite guinea pig. He calls him Mike Tyson, even though Mike Tyson is *clearly* a girl (because he just had a baby).

Corner Boy gets Mike Tyson and Mike Tyson's baby from his pocket.

'I can't talk!' I say. 'I have to go to school!'

'Why?'

'Detective work,' I tell him. 'Cassidy has been blamed for taking that money. If I can't find the thief, we'll never get that playground, and she *might go to prison*!'

Corner Boy's giving a mad stare through his thick glasses.

'I'll come with you!' he says. 'I'll get my spear.'

Corner Boy has a spear which he likes to carry around everywhere. He runs off to get it now.

I don't think I should do detective work with Corner Boy and Mike Tyson and Mike Tyson's baby.

It doesn't seem professional.

As Corner Boy comes back with the spear, my brother is coming out of the house.

'What are we waiting for?' he says, swaggering over. 'It's time for an *Out-on-bikes Adventure*!' He swings his back leg over the bike.

He cycles off.

Corner Boy and I cycle off behind him.

CHAPTER SEVEN:
An Out-on-bikes Adventure

Even though I am still very WORRIED about Cat, and I am very ANGRY about the theft, I can't help but feel HAPPY that we're out on bikes. You never feel bad on a bike.

As we
head off,
my brother
does his
tricks.

So I do tricks.

We all do tricks.

Then a pigeon poos on my brother's face. I laugh.

And then I smack the kerb. And I nearly smack into a person. It's Stephen Maysmith the police detective.

I can't believe it. He is walking along with Fiona McTavish, looking more important than I've ever seen him look.

'Mr Maysmith,' I ask. 'What are you doing?'
'I will shortly be giving a press conference,' he announces, 'on behalf of the police!'
Then I see something even more surprising.

The *Komodo dragon* comes plodding out into the First Years' playground. He's being led by Michael Mulligan's two men.

What are they doing?

'How will we get into the school?' I ask my brother.

'We need a diversion,' he says.

'You GO IN,' Corner Boy tells me. 'I will CREATE THE DIVERSION! Here . . . TAKE Mike Tyson and his baby.'

He passes me the guinea pigs. I put them in my pocket.

'What are you going to do?' I ask.

'Just WATCH,' says Corner Boy.

He throws down his bike. Then, holding up his spear, he SPRINTS towards the dragon, *roaring*.

Meanwhile . . .

I SPRINT into the school.

Luckily Mrs Daniels
is not there. Ten
seconds after Corner
Boy's diversion, I
push open the door to
Turkey-head's office.

Two seconds later, I have put the memory
stick down by her computer. *Done!*

I look at the walls of her office. I see several pictures of Ms Turkey-head with her slug-lip sister.

I am just thinking how alike the sisters actually look. Then something very BAD happens . . .

Mr Bolton comes in.

'*What are you doing here?*' he says, furious.
I think of something Mr Meeton taught
me in ping-pong: *Attack is the best form of
defence.*

I poke the Bolton in the chest.

'I'm here,' I tell him, 'because my friend has been BLAMED for stealing that money, and YOU'RE the one who had the key!'

'Are you accusing me?' he bellows. 'I would give my life to this school!'

I'm thinking: *He would!*

'You must have given the key TO someone!' I say.

I get an idea.

'Who was it?' I say. 'Was it *Michael Mulligan*? Did he *bribe* you?'

'How *dare* you!' he says. 'I have never given the key to anyone!'

'What, no one?'

'I gave it to Ms Birkinstead this morning – otherwise I've *never let it out of my sight*! And meanwhile I have already told you the school is CLOSED so YOU are about to get into a LOT OF TROUBLE!'

'I am a detective!' I tell Mr Bolton. 'I am not scared of TROUBLE!'

And I charge off towards trouble like
I'm a *triceratops*.

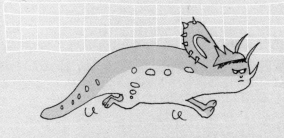

CHAPTER EIGHT:
On the Trail

Sixty seconds later, I'm back outside by the bikes. There's no sign of Corner Boy. But my brother is standing there, looking important.

'Well,' I tell him. 'I went in there and put back the memory stick! What have *you* done?'

'I have been following up some LEADS!' he says.

'What?' I say.

'I have been observing those men,' he says, pointing.

Nearby are Michael Mulligan's men, putting the *Komodo dragon* into the back of a van.

'The one on the left is called Guy "The Eyes" Murphy,' he says. 'The other is called Derek "Dent-head" O'Malley!'

'How do you know that?' I ask.

He gives me a proud, smug look.

'Dad told me,' he says.

'What?' I say. 'How would Dad know
men like that?' I so want to know more.

But just then the van drives past. As it does, the two men turn as one and face us.

'I *suggest* we follow them!' he says. 'Or *are you scared*?'

'*I'm* not scared!' I say. 'Are *you* scared?'

'No way, my little friend!' says my brother. 'I am NEVER SCARED!'

And then, sticking out his back leg (looking like a cat who's just had a pee), my brother mounts his bike.

And then as
he cycles along
– to *prove he's
not scared* – my
brother does
tricks.

So I then do tricks.

We both do tricks. The two men don't seem to notice us.

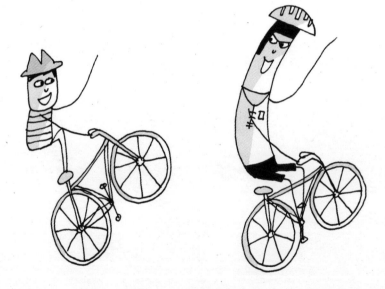

I suppose if you are criminals, you
expect to be followed by policemen in cars.

Or you expect to be followed by other criminals, who'd be riding motorbikes that would have jet-engines and special drones shaped like bats that would zoom into the car to film.

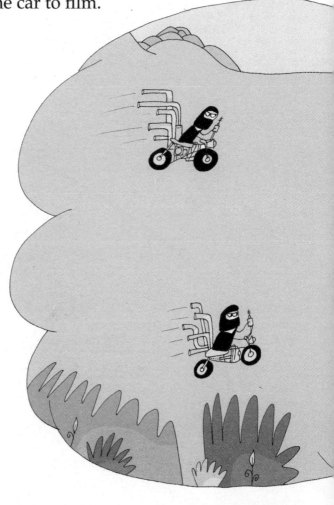

You don't expect to be followed by two
boys on bikes . . .

. . . especially if they're doing tricks (and one of them still has some pigeon poo on his face). We can't help it. It's just *fun* being on bikes.

Riding over the Michael Mulligan
Bridge, I see a hot-air balloon.

We are both in such good moods.

As we go *jiggle-jiggling* into the square
in the old town, the sun suddenly comes
out.

At the same time, two old bald fellers come out of the library and we give them a wave.

'If those guys were dinosaurs,' I ask my brother, 'what kind would they be?'

'Pachycephalosauruses,' he says. 'They were the ones with the thick reinforced skulls that they'd use to *smash* into other dinosaurs.'

'Are you saying,' I ask, 'that librarians might charge and smash into people with their specially thick skulls?'

'Librarians would *never* do that,' he says, 'unless you were writing in a library book.'

I actually laugh at that.

He's all right, my brother (for a muppet).

'What do you get,' I say, 'if you cross a dinosaur with a pig?'

'What?' he says.

'Jurassic Pork,' I say.

My brother laughs. I laugh.

As we go round the hilltop road
that has a view right over the sea, I am
thinking: *This is one of the best bike rides I've
ever done.*

But then we come to Michael Mulligan's huge house, and I suddenly GET THE FEAR.

CHAPTER NINE:
In the T-Rex's Lair

It's a huge scary *castle*. It has a moat round it, and there's a drawbridge, and a big gate that stays open after the black car sweeps through.

It's like this.

We leave our bikes in some nettles.

We peek through the entrance.
We can actually *see* Michael Mulligan.

183

With his back to us, he's sitting by a swimming pool that has a fountain in the shape of a gun.

His two men are talking to him, but it's *so annoying* – we can't *hear* what they're saying.

185

I look at my brother.

'Will we creep closer,' I whisper, 'or are you scared?'

'*I'm* not scared!' he whispers (very quietly). 'Are *you*?'

'No!' I say.

'So let's creep closer,' he whispers.

We both crawl forward like lizards.

As we do, we realise there is a *real* lizard on the loose. And it's a *KOMODO DRAGON.*

My brother hides behind a barbecue. I crouch behind a bag of coal.

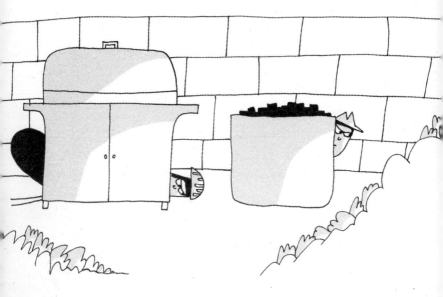

I can now *hear* Guy 'The Eyes' Murphy as he speaks to Mulligan . . .

'We think he ate something unusual,' says The Eyes.

'As long as he didn't eat a teacher,' says Mulligan.

What are they talking about? I strain my head forward, *needing* to hear. But then something TERRIBLE happens.

Mike Tyson's baby crawls out of my pocket. He's snuffling around on the grass.

And something notices.

It's the *Komodo dragon*. He reaches out his long tongue. *This is awful.*

I stretch towards the guinea pig.

And that's how I knock over the big bag of coal.

Mulligan turns slowly in my direction.

'Rory Branagan,' he says in his low,
rumbling voice. 'How kind of you to
come!'

'How do you know who I am?' I say (sounding squeaky).

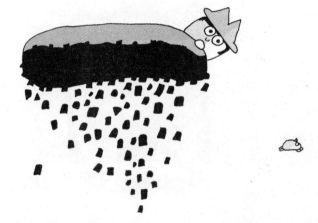

Mulligan looks at me.

'That's for me to know,' he says, 'and
for you *not* to find out.'

Suddenly the *Komodo dragon* lashes his giant tongue out towards me, and I'm so scared I could die.

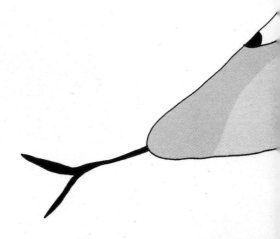

'Mr Mulligan,' I squeak. 'Do you think you could call off the dragon?'

'I wouldn't worry about him,' says Mulligan. 'He's been away for a while and we've just given him a whole weekend's worth of food.'

I'm thinking: *That is an odd thing to say!*

Even though I am so scared, I am
thinking: *I still need to be a detective.*

'Are you saying,' I ask, 'that the dragon
has been away for the whole weekend?'

'We left him in the school,' says Mulligan.

'What?' I say. 'You let your dragon stay in the school?!'

'We didn't *let* him,' says Mulligan. 'We just kind of . . . *forgot* him. He spent the weekend behind the school boiler, trying to keep warm.'

'Do you mean to say,' I ask, 'that this dragon has spent the weekend in *Ms Birkinstead's office*?'

'That's right!' says Mulligan, and he *gives a mysterious smile*. 'Which should have stopped most people stealing the money.'

As I look up at his face, I am thinking: *I don't care how powerful he is. I am going to get to the bottom of this!*

I am a detective, I think. I wouldn't care if I had to face the biggest T-Rex of all.

If it was guarding a MYSTERY,
I would still face up to it.

'Did YOU steal that money?' I ask.

Mulligan looks at me as if he's wondering which part of me to eat first.

'I promised to MATCH the school's money, and to GIVE my own,' he says. 'So why would I be stealing?'

'Because it would stop you having to pay up,' I say. 'And because you are a criminal!'

Should I have said that?

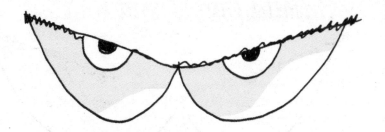

I am now looking right into Michael
Mulligan's *T-Rex* eyes.

Oh my God, I am SO SCARED now!
But . . .
Suddenly . . .

... *he laughs!*

'I *AM the most deadly CRIMINAL of all*!' he says. 'But stealing money that some kids have raised for their school – whoever did that is a total SCUMBAG, and if I find out who they are, I will rip the pipes from their stomach and wear them like a scarf!'

Mulligan's smile suddenly disappears.

'And if you don't leave my house now, *I will do that to you.*'

I say nothing.

'And that goes for your brother too!' he says.

'Who do you mean?' I say.

'I can see his skinny butt sticking out from that barbecue,' he says. 'And he better remove it,

NOWWWWW!'

And Michael Mulligan *ROARS*.

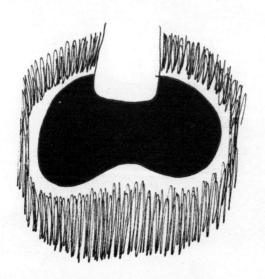

Terrified, I scoop up the guinea pig. I run off. My brother runs too. We run right out of the gate and across the moat.

CHAPTER TEN:
A New Level of Fear

Then my brother suddenly stops running.

'I wasn't scared at all!' he says.

'Nor was I!' I tell him. 'I did not think he would hurt us!'

'*I also don't think Mulligan took that money!*' says my brother.

'But,' I reply, 'Mr Bolton said the only person who's had the key was Ms Birkinstead!'

My brother gives me his most *detectivey* face.

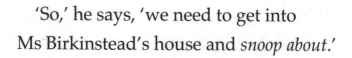

'So,' he says, 'we need to get into Ms Birkinstead's house and *snoop about.*'

I don't like the idea of that at all. Even just thinking about that makes me feel as if I'm going to faint. The whole world seems **white.**

'How do you even know where she lives?' I ask.

'Don't you remember when we had to go to bible class with Mr Birkinstead?' says my brother.

'What?' I say. 'Noah the Nostril?'

'EXACTLY!' says my brother. 'Him!'

'What's he got to do with
Ms Birkinstead?'

'He's called *Mr Birkinstead*,' says my
brother. 'That is what we detectives call a
CLUE!'

And then my brother picks up his bike and swings his back leg even higher this time.

Then he rides off.

I'd say my brother and I are both RELIEVED we got away from Mulligan without being eaten alive. But I am still *terrified* that we're going to have to break into Ms Turkey-head's house.

As we ride round the hilltop road, I wish big *pterosaurs* might swoop down and carry me off, so we never have to arrive.

As we speed through the town square past the librarians, I'm thinking: *I wish they WERE Pachycephalosauruses. I wish they WOULD charge us with their thick skulls, so we'd be forced to DODGE them, then FIGHT them using our bikes as weapons.*

I'm thinking: *I wish* ANYTHING *could be happening, because* NOTHING *could be as bad as having to go to* SNOOP ABOUT IN MY HEAD TEACHER'S HOUSE.

Far too soon, we arrive at the house Ms Birkinstead shares with Noah the Nostril. (We called him that because he was OBSESSED with Noah, and had the biggest nostrils you'd ever seen.)

We swing off the bikes.

I definitely do not want to go in. I am

SO NERVOUS.

But my brother is just cockily looking at the front of the building.

'I'll do the talking!' he says.

I say, 'Thanks.'

'The first-floor window is open,' he says.
'You just have to climb the drainpipe.'

I DEFINITELY don't like the sound of
this!

'What?' I say.
'Why am I climbing in?'
'Well, if *I'm* doing the
talking,' he says, '*you* have
to do the snooping.'

He looks at me. I look at him.
I so **HATE** him now.

Then I look at the window. It seems to get *higher* each time I see it.

'You scared?' he says.
'No!' I tell him.

'Good,' he says. 'Why don't you hide behind the bin while I ring the doorbell?'

As he goes to ring the bell, I am getting even more scared.

But then I am thinking: *I NEED to find the school's money because I NEED to rescue Cat.* Then I look at the window, which seems to have got HIGHER still.

But in my mind
the Cat is up there,
waiting to be rescued.

Then I'm thinking…
It wouldn't matter
if that window was
higher than the
Empire State
Building . . .

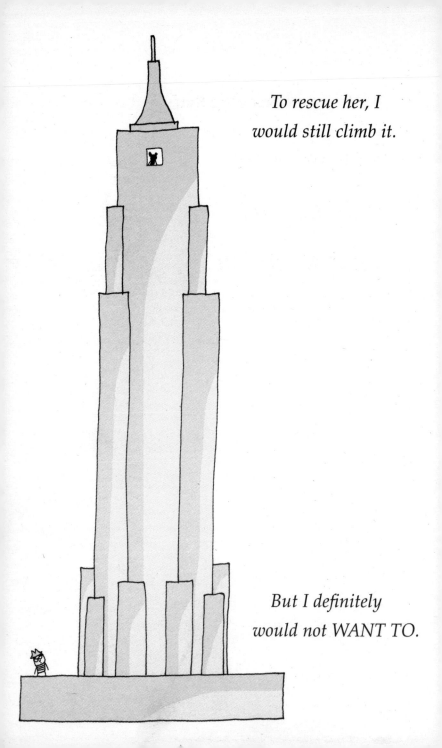

To rescue her, I would still climb it.

But I definitely would not WANT TO.

And, as I am thinking that, my brother *rap-rap-raps* on the door.

Noah opens it.

*(Oh my God, I had forgotten just how **big** those nostrils are!)*

'Yes?' he says.

'Mr Birkinstead,' says my brother, 'I need extra bible classes.'

'Why?' he says.

My brother gives him a fierce look.

'*I have felt the call,*' he says.

(Fair play to him!)

Noah gives a long, hard stare down his nostrils. (*My God, they are big! You wouldn't be surprised to find a family of sparrows up there, eating worms!*)

'Come in,' he says.

The door shuts,
and, praying I will
not fall, I climb.

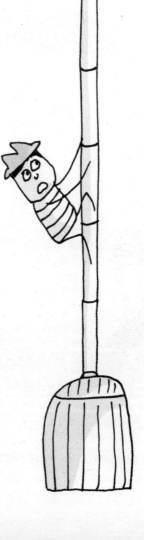

A few seconds later, I am on the ledge.

A bit of brick falls and smashes on the steps. Looking down, I've *never been so scared*.

Fingers trembling, I reach for the window. Now I'm *terrified* someone will see me.

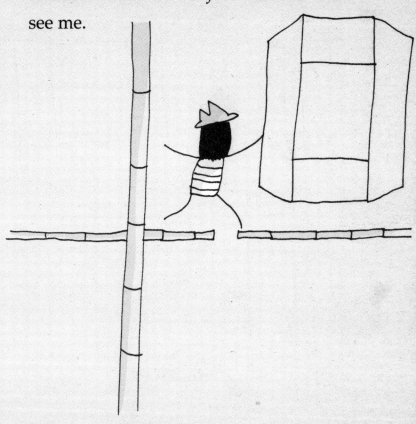

Shaking, I step across.

Then

I

flop

inside . . .

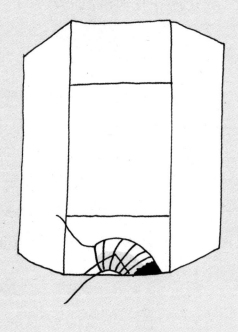

CHAPTER ELEVEN:
The Turkey's Secret

Looking up, I see I've landed right in
Ms Turkey-head's bedroom. It smells of
head teacher. By the bed, there's the make-up
she smears on her face.

All around the room, Ms Birkinstead's outfits are hanging like lots of dangling head teachers, but she's not here.

I'm trying to imagine where she might have hidden the money.

One cupboard is slightly open. As I go
over, the floor CREAKS.

Inside, there are head-teacher shoes on
the floor. *If you want to understand someone,*
Mrs Welkin always says, *walk a mile in
their shoes.* (I'm thinking… *Should I put on
Ms Turkey-head's shoes?*)

Then I see her head.

I
J
U
M
P.

I open the cupboard further and . . .

. . . I see it's just a dummy head that *has
a wig*. I'm thinking... *I didn't know she wore
a wig!*

I'm thinking… *Should I put on her shoes, her wig and some of her clothes? That way, if Noah the Nostril comes in, he might think I'm her?* I actually CONSIDER that for a moment.

Then I think: *Actually . . . Best not.*

But just imagining Ms Turkey-head makes me realise: *I DID see her at the school this morning . . .*

And I DID see her on the CCTV . . .

DID she STEAL THAT MONEY?

And, if so, WHERE DID SHE PUT IT?

On a high shelf, I see loads of files.
One says: *Mouse Class 2015*. I was in
that class. I take the file down.

I find a picture.

I see me and Corner Boy dressed as
Batman and Robin.

I turn over pages and find another
picture that gets my attention.

It's Dad!

I read:

'The police have requested that if
Padder Branagan tries to approach Rory,
they should be called. His presence could
be bad for Rory. It could also be bad for
the whole school . . .'

I'm thinking . . . *WHY would it be BAD for the entire school if my dad came?*

I'm thinking . . . *It will be a lot WORSE if I can't find this money! We'll never repair ANYTHING and the whole place will just COLLAPSE.*

I put the file back. I have to wiggle it.
And that's how I knock something
down from the top of the pile.

It's a pink tin.

It CLONKS me on the head.

And as it does . . .

. . . Big *pterosaur* thoughts come
SWOOPING into my
head. I'm thinking:

I have the stolen tin right here!

Which means . . .

. . . MY HEAD TEACHER IS A THIEF!

Then I'm thinking:

I am GOING TO BRING HER DOWN!

But the trouble is I also
realise I just made a big bang,
then said 'Ow!'

Did Noah the Nostril hear? I listen
carefully.

'Is someone there?' he calls.

Silence. I'm not answering that.

But then I hear him coming.

Pulling the cupboard door shut, I press myself back into Ms Birkinstead's jackets.

Oh no, I think, *please please please don't let Noah find me!*

Suddenly, he YANKS the doors open,
and I'm staring up into his nostrils.

Lord, they are big!

(You wouldn't be surprised to find a family of cavemen up there, painting the walls!)

'*What are you doing?*' he snarls. He sees the tin, and looks about to GRAB IT.

And *that*'s what starts the ACTION.

CHAPTER TWELVE:
Action — Fast, Lethal Action

I push Nostril in the belly with the tin.

'Give that back here,' he says as I dodge
from the cupboard. 'It's ours!'

'Oh, so you ADMIT it, do you?' I snarl.

'You *admit* your wife TOOK the school's money? *She's a THIEF!'*

'GIVE BACK THAT TIN!' he roars.

He *lunges*.

But I just *skip* fast round the bed. He skips too. The pair of us are skipping like a couple of dancers. He then LEAPS at me again. But he's too slow.

I just SPRING up on the bed, then I *bounce* and I *boing* down the other side. I back away to the door . . .

. . . But just then someone barges through. It's Ms Birkinstead.

It is said that turkeys and chickens are the animals most closely related to the dinosaurs. *Definitely* . . . Ms Turkey-head gives me her most *velociraptor-like* look.

'*Rory Branagan!*' she says. 'What are *you* doing in my house?'

But I'm NOT SCARED OF HER!

'*Ms Birkinstead*,' I say right back, 'what the HECK are YOU doing stealing the school's money?'

'How could I have stolen the money?' she says. 'I've been away on my course!'

As I look at her, I so nearly believe her.

'I've only just come back!' she says.

'But I know you're lying,' I say. 'I have the money *right here*!' I say.

'That's *not* the money!' she says.

'I *know* this is the money!' I say.

And I rip off the lid of the tin.

And I see it's full of Ms Birkinstead's pants!

That is a sight you SHOULD NEVER
HAVE TO SEE! I am so *embarrassed*.

'But I thought this was the tin with the
money,' I say.

'There are quite a few tins like that!' she
says. 'Who doesn't like those biscuits?'

I am about to go out of the door when I get a most *detectivey thought*.

'But,' I say, 'if you've only just come back from the course, then . . . WHO THE HECK WAS AT THE SCHOOL THIS MORNING AND *TOOK THE KEY FROM MR BOLTON?*'

'What?' she says. She is looking at me in *total confusion*.

And, as I look back at her, I definitely know how she feels.

If she was not at school this morning, I am thinking, *then WHO THE HECK WAS THAT ON THE CCTV?* And, as I try to answer that question, for a moment my mind is as blank as a big wall of ice.

And the next moment . . .

... BIG THOUGHTS come LEAPING in like penguins.

I think ...

I think ...

I think . . . *I HAVE SOLVED THE CASE!!! (And my brother hasn't!)*

I sprint out of the room.

I'm about to sprint out of the house
when I remember him.

'Are you coming?' I call.
My brother emerges from the kitchen.

'What were you *doing*?' I ask.

'Just eating biscuits,' he says, 'and reading the Book of Jonah.'

'What happens?' I ask.

'It's all about this old feller Jonah who's eaten by a whale. But in the end he gets out.'

I ask, 'What happens to the whale?'

'I don't know,' he says.

'He's probably hiding,' I say, 'up Noah's nose!'

We both laugh.

We are about to go.

But the Birkinsteads now appear at the top of the stairs.

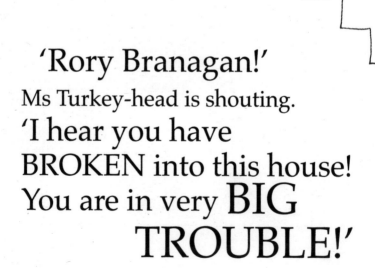

'Rory Branagan!'
Ms Turkey-head is shouting.
'I hear you have
BROKEN into this house!
You are in very BIG
TROUBLE!'

'Why don't you report me to the POLICE?' I suggest (eyes gleaming).

'I might just do that!' she says.

'They're at the school!' I tell her. 'I should get over there! The real thief is about to be unmasked!'

'What do you mean?' says Ms Turkey-head. 'Who is it?'

'*Follow the detectives!*' I shout. 'We are about to SWOOP!'

And my brother and I shoot out of the door.

CHAPTER THIRTEEN:
The Press Conference

We don't mess about. We get the bikes
and *speed off to school*. The Birkinsteads
stop behind us at some traffic lights at one
point and Noah leaps out to GET US.

I turn round and he's coming at us like a zombie again – nostrils *quivering* – as if he means to *catch us in them*.

He *so nearly* catches us too. But then the lights change.

Next thing my brother and I are OFF,
wiggling our bums in his face.

After that the road goes downhill and
we get WAY AHEAD.

Soon we are *shooting* down towards the school. I can see it all . . .

The press conference is a bit like the Big Presentation Event. I can see the little stage where Stephen Maysmith is standing beside Fiona McTavish.

I can see two TV cameras and a screen that's showing live TV. I can see a crowd

gathered in the playground.

And at the back, near the gate, I can see a very posh woman standing with a sneery expression on her face. It's Slug Lip – Ms Birkinstead's sister – *the head teacher of the King George School.*

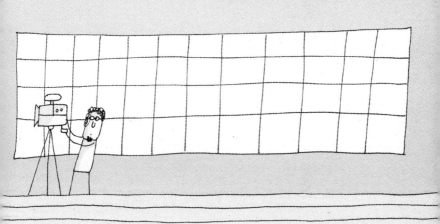

I sidle up to her.

'What are YOU looking at?' she says.

'I know YOU took our money!' I say.

'So why don't I *have* your money?'
she says, and she gives me an EVIL,
JEALOUS LOOK.

'I'm going to GET YOU,' I snarl.

She moves off. I am about to follow her.

But I'm stopped by Ms Turkey-head.
'Rory,' she hisses, 'you do NOT break
into people's houses!'

'Your sister stole our money,' I tell her.
She looks at me. And, as she does, I see
she did not know. But she's definitely not
surprised.

'Your sister is EVIL,' I tell her. 'She thinks her school should have *everything* and ours should have NOTHING, and YOU are just *letting it happen.*'

'Trust me,' she says. 'I am not.'

'What are you doing?' I demand.

'Quiet!' she warns. She nods towards the stage. I see the press conference has started.

Stephen Maysmith is onstage.

'And the police would like to REASSURE the public,' he is saying, 'that within moments of the money being stolen, the police were here. And they immediately *caught a suspect*.'

I can't help it.

'YES!' I shout.

'But it was
the *wrong one!*'

Everyone looks at me, but no one
believes me. *Still . . .* I think. *At least I've
got their attention.* I now walk up on to
the stage.

And I point out the Slug Lip like I'm pointing out a witch.

'SHE took it!' I say. 'Her – the head teacher of the King George School! She was JEALOUS because our fete was so brilliant. She dressed up as her sister, and she STOLE THE MONEY!'

'Nonsense,' says Slug Lip. 'I don't have your money!'

'You took it!' I say. 'And I will PROVE IT!'

I turn to Fiona McTavish.

'Take your cameras,' I tell her. 'Go to the office. Tell Mr Bolton to put in the memory stick with *CCTV* Sellotaped to it. And press *play*.'

I look at Stephen Maysmith. He's saying nothing.

I see I'm basically running this press conference. I *so* hope I'm right.

Up on the screen, we watch as Fiona McTavish goes back into school. To my horror, I realise that this is on live TV, so it's being watched by thousands of people.

I'm thinking: *I so hope I'm right, or this could be very embarrassing.*

The camera goes past Mrs Daniels. It goes towards Ms Turkey-head's office . . .

. . . and, as it does, I'm still thinking of the Slug Lip saying: *'Why don't I have your money?'*

And the pterosaurs are swooping in my head now.

I'm thinking . . .

So WHY does Slug Lip not have the money?

I'm thinking . . .

Have I GOT THIS ALL WRONG?

I'm thinking . . .

Am I about to make the BIGGEST, MOST EMBARRASSING MISTAKE OF MY LIFE???

But then I notice the *dent on the door,* and I think:

I KNOW WHAT HAPPENED and *I HAVE SOLVED THE CASE!*

On camera, Mr Bolton finds the memory stick. He puts it into the computer. The camera goes in close on to the screen. *Everyone* is hoping to see final evidence of the Big Cash Robbery . . .

. . . but the thief does not appear.

Instead . . . *I do*! My face *fills* the screen.
I SHOUT: '*Big Bad Bolton Man! I said*
Big Bad Bolton Man! (Uh huh huh.)'

At first people can't believe it. Then one
second later, the whole school *creases* up
with laughter.

Next, I am upside down. Bouncing up and down like a lizard on the ceiling, I am going: *'Big Bad Bolton Man . . . I say YOU, my Bolton Man! (Oh yeah!)'*

The whole school is laughing now. I am scared Fiona McTavish will cut off the camera.

LUCKILY, *right then*, someone else appears on the monitor.

And it *looks* like Ms Birkinstead. She
has Ms Birkinstead's jacket. She has
Ms Birkinstead's hair.

On-screen, the *head teacher of the King George School* opens the door of the safe. She is SO BUSTED. *You can clearly see her slug lip as she takes out the big pink tin.* She is ready to go, but JUST THEN the *actual thief* appears from behind the boiler . . .

. . . and it's a very big *Komodo dragon*! It sticks out its tongue.

The head teacher turns. She *screams*. She chucks the tin at the dragon.

She *sprints* out of the door. Behind her, the dragon puts the tin in its mouth. He can't get it down his throat.

So he CHARGES head-first at the door.

Bang!

He hits that door so hard he leaves a
dent, and he *swallows the tin*.

Fiona McTavish appears on the TV.

'It's not often that a crime is solved live on air.' She smiles. 'But it was just now . . . Back to the studio.'

CHAPTER FOURTEEN:
An Epic Ending

Outside, some people cheer. Others boo.

'The King George School is EVIL!' shouts Duncan Cliffhead. 'Let's go and *BURN IT DOWN!*'

Someone needs to take control.

Someone does.

It's Ms Birkinstead.

She gives everyone her most velociraptor-like GLARE.

We all go quiet.

'I do *not* want you thinking the King George School is evil,' she says. 'In fact, only this week they have agreed to let us – *free of charge* – use their football fields, swimming pools and diving board . . .'

As I look at Slug Lip, who is standing at the back of the crowd, I see this was the first *she* knew of the deal.

But she *definitely* says NOTHING.
And that's the moment Stephen Maysmith grabs her.

And suddenly the sun is coming out, and most of us are thinking: *Ah, Ms Turkey-head is not so bad. She's just given us swimming pools and diving boards. She can stay on as head!*

But Corner Boy is still just thinking about the penguins.

'But,' he shouts, 'will we still be getting the ADVENTURE PLAYGROUND?'

'Well, that depends on Mr Mulligan,' says Ms Birkinstead.

And she looks towards the back of the crowd. *Everyone* now looks at the back of the crowd. Michael Mulligan is there.

'Since my dragon ate the money,' he rumbles, 'I will still give you the five-point-three million. You can choose what to turn the Old Factory into. Just call it . . . the Michael Mulligan *Dragon Zone.*'

He smiles a lethal smile.

'Do you accept?' he says.

'I accept,' says Ms Birkinstead. And now the whole school sees something we've never seen before . . .

She smiles.

And it's a very nice smile.

'So I suggest,' she says, 'that we cancel the rest of the day's lessons, so we can all go to the King George School and have a jolly good swim!'

And now it's like a *volcano of happiness* goes off in the playground.

'YESSSSSSSSSS!'

we all roar. Right away, everyone is RUNNING for the King George School, ready to swim.

I am about to run myself.

But then someone taps me on the shoulder.

I turn.

I see someone.

And she's got a big grin, and she's wearing pyjamas.

Cat smiles.

'Deadly Branagan!' she says. 'You just solved another crime!'

I am *so* pleased she's back.

'But I couldn't have done it,' I tell her, 'if you hadn't knocked down Slug Lip and got the CCTV footage! How did you even *know* to suspect her?'

As Cassidy smiles, I have never seen her look more cat-like.

'That's for me to know,' she says, 'and you not to find out. Because right now, I need a swim!'

We all go – me, Cat, my brother and
Corner Boy too.

And in no time at all, we arrive at the
King George School. Loads of people are
there already. No one has even bothered to

go home for their proper swimming things.
They're all just *bombing* into the pool,
dressed in boxers or rolled-up trousers.

I go up to the top of the tallest diving board with my brother. My God, it's a LONG way down!

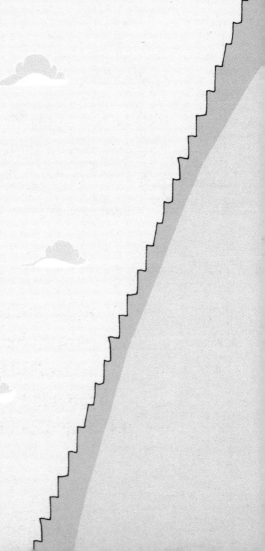

'Would you be scared to
jump that?' says my brother.
    I have to tell him.
    'I would!' I say. I don't like
to admit it, but I do.

'I thought you *never* got scared!' he says.

'Actually,' I say, 'I have been scared all day!'

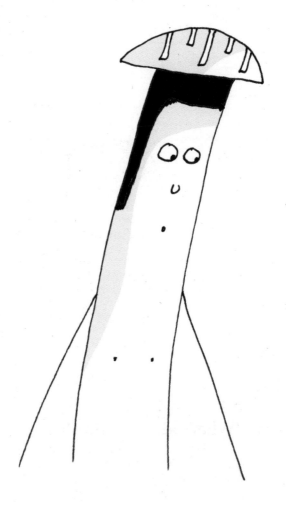

'So have I,' he says. 'But we've done some mad stuff today: if we weren't scared, we'd be stupid. But you know what they always say?'

I say, 'What?'

'It's all right to be scared,' says my brother. 'But still . . . at some point, you have to LEAP ahead anyway – and that's what you've done today.'

As I look at my brother, I'm thinking: *WHY is he still wearing his BIKE HELMET?*

I'm thinking: *My brother is such an EEJIT. But he's definitely not a CRIMINAL. And he did help me today. And he's actually been good fun.*

'Seamus,' I say. 'Thanks for today.'

'It's OK!' he says, and then suddenly I am SO EMBARRASSED, and I actually just want to *push him off the diving board.*

But I don't. *(Give me credit! I don't!)*

I just turn away, and I look over the big
field of people all having a good time, and
I think: *we helped make that happen*, and I
feel so proud I could burst.

I see Cat with Corner Boy. He's showing her Mike Tyson's baby. I see Stephen Maysmith. He's just walking around, looking important but eating some custard creams.

'Will we bomb him?' I ask my brother.

'Well, I am Senior Brother,' he says.

'And I say: *We will!*'

I laugh, a bit.

I then look over the side one last time, and I think: *My Lord, it's a long way down!* But then I think: *It is still a once-in-a-lifetime opportunity to bomb Stephen Maysmith.*

Smiling, I turn to my brother.
I hold out my hand.
He smiles. He holds out his.

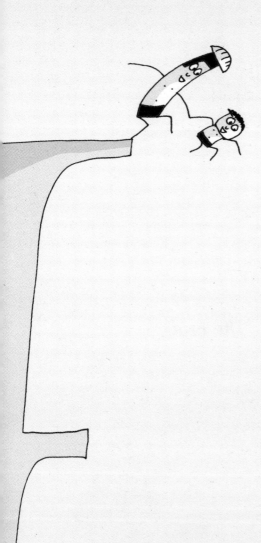

And then, together, we *LEAP*.

The End

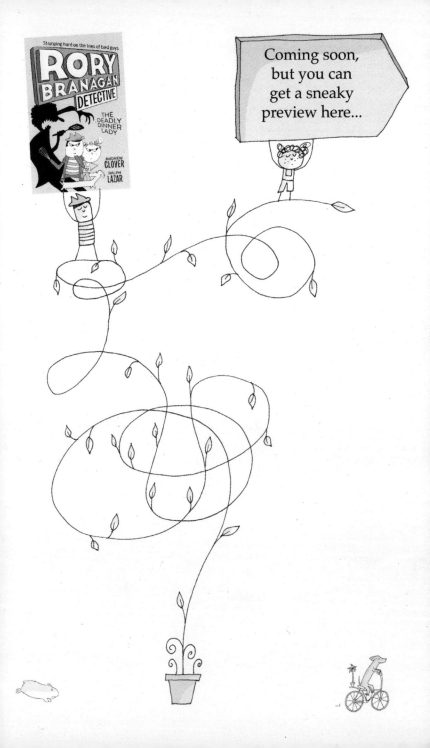

RORY BRANAGAN DETECTIVE
THE DEADLY DINNER LADY
Stamping hard on the toes of bad guys.
ANDREW CLOVER
RALPH LAZAR

Coming soon, but you can get a sneaky preview here...

There comes a time in the life of any schoolchild when we must leave the land of the teachers, to go . . .

. . . into the lair of the dinner ladies.

We go into the canteen and they come out of the kitchen, all scowling and steaming like dragons.

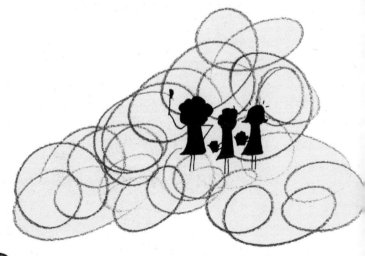

The first one is called Ms Lineham, but we call her Ms Slimer because she looks like a big slug.

The second is called Mrs Winscombe.

No one has ever heard her speak. And
the third . . .

. . . is Ms Dinefield, the most gorgeous
dinner lady in the whole wide world.

Everyone is in love with her.

Even Mr Meeton.

And I think she likes him (because he is the coolest teacher by a mile).

And Mr Bolton likes her too.

He spends all lunchtime standing
behind her, guarding her like a big dog.
He doesn't even notice anymore if you try
to sneak an extra yoghurt.

But Ms Slimer does.

If you even touch her yoghurts, she'll grab them off you, and she'll be spitting: 'Don't you touch my yoghurts! You horrible boy!'

She hates everyone. And – I can hardly bear to say this – but I must . . .

Everyone hates Ms Slimer.

I'm so sorry to say it, but they do.

But who would actually want to kill her? That is the question.

And how?

And why?

Because that's what happens.

I'll tell you the whole story . . .

To be continued . . .